ARE MIRACLES *for* REAL?

ARE MIRACLES *for* REAL?

You Be the Judge

MARIA BAAN

ARE MIRACLES FOR REAL?
YOU BE THE JUDGE

Photo credit: www.ericstephenjacobs.com

iUniverse books may be ordered through booksellers or by contacting:

iUniverse
1663 Liberty Drive
Bloomington, IN 47403
www.iuniverse.com
1-800-Authors (1-800-288-4677)

ISBN: 978-1-5320-8176-7 (sc)
ISBN: 978-1-5320-8177-4 (e)

Library of Congress Control Number: 2019914027

Print information available on the last page.

iUniverse rev. date: 12/26/2019

Contents

PART II
Miracles in the Entertainment Field

PART III
Me, a Grandmother?

Introduction

My reason for writing this book is to encourage and give hope to anyone who will read the stories. This is a collection of miracles; some of the stories are written by the person who experienced the miracle, and others are written by me. When you read these stories, my prayer is that you will come to know the truth of God's love for the world. Please note this is not about how perfect Maria is; no, it is about a perfect God who loves you just as you are.

Hometown Girl Bio

You might wonder how a hometown girl like me landed up in two unexpected life paths—one as a nurse, and the other as an actress. Even as a child, I was obsessed with performing, and I always had a heart for suffering people, which led me to become a nurse.

As fate would have it, I fell in love and was married and divorced with a beautiful baby girl named Annmarie by the time I was twenty-four. This presented a plethora of situations that challenged me to the max. As my acting dreams shifted to the back burner, I was faced with being a working single parent of a two-year-old while attending nursing school. I had a lot of help with the babysitting, thank God!

While supporting my daughter, I would usually take on every type of nursing job, such as private duty, hospitals, and nursing homes.

Occasionally I would try other types of jobs, such as the time I answered an ad from an exclusive New York agency for a position as a tour guide. Incredibly, they were offering $250 per hour to accompany a wealthy client on a tour around New York. I couldn't wait to meet my client, Edward, who I thought was visiting New York and was staying in a lavish apartment on the Upper East Side. Upon meeting Edward, he immediately asked if I would like have a glass of champagne. I sat down and said, "No thank you." *What have I gotten myself into?* I thought.

"Where will we be going tonight?" I asked. "Will we be going to dinner and the theatre?"

He laughed at me and said, "You are kidding, right?"

I said, "No, I'm hungry. I thought we were going out on the town and to dinner."

He said, "Honey, you could afford to shed a few pounds." He promptly grabbed the phone and yelled at the agency, "Don't ever send me another newbie; she really thinks she's going to be a tour guide. I'm only paying for one hour!" He tossed his credit card across the table and said, "Get whatever you want and bring me back my card."

Actually, it was the best meal I'd had in a long time. I ate at the restaurant across the street and delivered his card back as he requested—and immediately ran out the door.

I *really* thought I was going to be a tour guide.

I still do not know why I tried working with this agency two more times before I realized all of the guys had unrealistic expectations—at least as far as I was concerned.

Needless to say, the agency figured out they would be losing money if they kept sending me out. A word to the wise: if it sounds too good to be true, it probably is.

My acting dream continued to simmer. While working as a nurse at a local hospital, I was tempted by the possibility of auditioning for a movie. I leapt at it. It was a *Saturday Night Fever* parody called *Nocturna*—a disco horror movie. The director assumed I had been in *Saturday Night Fever* and asked me to twirl around and dance. He hired me on the spot. I was hooked. It was my first acting job, as part of which I did a solo dance number, and I loved every minute of it.

It was a little complicated running into New York City every time I had to audition. Eventually I had to leave the regimented working schedule of a hospital and move into private-duty work.

I also added "set nurse" to my résumé and enjoyed working on movies and TV series with Liam Neeson, Dennis Leary, Kevin Bacon, Vincent D'Onofrio, James Spader, etc. Some amazing miracles occurred on the sets.

While working at a local hospital, a friend from Dietary invited me to a Bible study at her church. I decided to go, even though I had never been to a Bible study class and didn't know what to expect.

I went to the church in Patchogue, where I met my friend and was greeted by a very friendly group who welcomed me with open arms.

The pastor of the church, Pastor Benny, invited me up to the front and asked me if this was the first time I had been there.

I said, "Yes."

He asked me if he could pray with me.

I said, "Yes, Pastor, that would be fine."

While my eyes were closed, he began to pray.

I started to cry.

Pastor Benny said, "You have a big heart, and God is going to use you in a healing ministry."

While still sobbing, I slowly returned to my seat.

This experience was so far outside of my comfort zone; I didn't know what to think!

It left a lasting impression on me.

PART I

The Miracles

In the following pages, I have selected some of my favorite miracles to share. They are not in any chronological order except for the first one, which was my first encounter with the miraculous.

Blinded Motorcyclist Receives Sight

Within a couple of weeks of the Pastor Benny service, the spirit moved me. While working as a nurse at a nursing home, my heart was moved by a blind man who had completely lost his sight during a motorcycle accident many years earlier. He was now in his early forties, and the doctors said he would be totally blind for life. I asked if I could say a little prayer for him while placing my hand over his eyes. He agreed and said he felt heat. The severity of this situation caused me to run out of the room with my med cart to the nursing station, and then I ran into the bathroom crying.

The head nurse saw my state and said she would get me coverage and sent me home to rest for the day.

I returned to work a couple of days later and checked up on him. It was a miracle! He was starting to see shadows. Within a month, his vision was completely restored. I was subsequently let go because of my oversensitivity. They said I was too emotional and should not pursue this type of work. It's kind of ironic, isn't it? I went back to Pastor Benny looking for answers to this newfound ability through Christ, and he assured me that it was just the beginning. How right he was!

Eventually different gifts started to emerge. I became aware of a small inaudible voice inside prompting me to give total strangers a word. It frightened me at first to follow through. I thought I was losing it. After a while, I realized that the voice never seemed to be wrong. The ability to know in advance certain situations about total strangers and even global events began to develop.

God had blessed me with His healing grace and prophetic word. Thank you Jesus.

God Gives (Life-Long Atheist) A New Leg And Foot

This is my brother Bill's story in his own words.

On December 8, 2017, I noticed what looked like a small paper cut on the bottom of my left foot. I wasn't alarmed. Little did I know this would be a life-changing event, because I was a diabetic. This condition quickly progressed to the total destruction of my left leg and foot, reminiscent of a character in the TV show *The Walking Dead*, with loose, dangling flesh exposing blackened bone. My friends begged me to go to the nearest hospital. To this day, I don't know why I didn't go sooner. I think about this all the time. It was insane, and I have no reasonable explanation why I didn't go.

On January 9, 2018, I collapsed in my home and was unable to get up. I called my sister Maria, and she brought her daughter, Annmarie. This was the first time she had heard about my foot and the first time she had seen the mangled flesh that had once been my foot. They called an ambulance, and I was taken to the nearest hospital.

Before long I was taken to the operating room, where the surgeons worked on my leg and foot. When I was back in my room the surgeons informed me that I needed to have my leg amputated below the knee.

I was in a state of shock.

They had to move quickly.

They gave me no hope.

The leg had to come off.

It was not possible to save my leg under any circumstance.

My sister Maria loudly stated, "You are not getting your leg amputated." The doctors and nurses looked at her as if she were crazy.

Maria didn't budge. All she kept repeating was "If Jesus could raise three people from the dead, He can give you a new leg and foot."

Maria had me transferred to a nursing facility. The nursing facility originally said they would try to repair my leg and foot. After several weeks, they informed me that there was not any way to undo the tremendous damage and they couldn't save my leg and foot.

I was crushed for a second time.

Maria stood her ground. She prayed and kept repeating, "The Lord will get you the best surgeon, and your leg and foot will be restored."

Well, my sister was right! God sent me the best: Dr. John Kannengieser, a podiatrist from West Islip, New York. Dr. Kannengieser took on this challenge with extreme talent, dedication, and compassion. He did what no other surgeon would even attempt.

Slowly, over time, new tissue formed. Mangled flesh was replaced with healthy tissue and smooth skin. I was amazed. I asked Dr. Kannengieser if he had ever seen a wound like this heal the way this wound had.

Dr. Kannengieser looked at me, chuckled, and said, "Never!"

I was discharged from the nursing home with my newly repaired leg and foot—no amputation needed!

I know now there is a God, and I do believe in Jesus Christ. I also know my sister Maria doesn't reside in la-la land.

Follow-Up

My brother Bill's leg and foot are completely healed, with skin like a baby's. He no longer has diabetes. He weaned himself off of insulin by eating healthy foods and cutting down on calories.

His doctor ordered blood work to test blood sugar levels and was amazed everything was normal. He is no longer in danger. He lost seventy-five pounds, is walking on his foot, and is continuing to lose weight. Hallelujah!

My Ex-Husband's Wife Needed a Major Miracle

I can remember it as though it were yesterday. Something was disturbing my daughter, Annmarie. She finally got up the nerve to ask me if she and I could pray for my ex-husband's wife, Donna. He was Annmarie's father, and she was very concerned about something.

Donna and I always got along well. Joe and Donna had been married a few years and had not been successful in conceiving, though they very much wanted to have a child together.

Annmarie asked if we could visit Donna, and I said, "Sure, let's go."

Before long we were at Donna's front door. When Donna opened the door, she intuitively knew we had come there to pray for her.

She blurted out, "I don't pray the way you do."

Smiling, I said, "Aren't you going to invite us in for coffee?"

She chuckled and said, "Come in."

Always the perfect hostess, she served fresh-brewed coffee and fabulous homemade pastries as we sat around the living room coffee table. As Donna was questioning Annmarie about junior high, I gently took her hand and silently prayed for their fertility.

Shortly thereafter we said thank you and bade her good-bye.

Several weeks later, I received an unexpected call from my ex-husband Joe.

He could hardly speak. He was overwhelmed with untypical emotion. He repeatedly asked me, "Did you pray for Donna?"

I said, "Yes, I did."

He exclaimed, "She is pregnant!"

I said, "God answered the prayer. Thank you, Lord!"

Joe blurted out a few times, "You don't understand!'

I said, "What don't I understand?"

"The baby is due on *your* birthday!"

We both cried for joy.

Miracle on Thirty-Fourth Street

It was one of those days when I had just gotten in from Long Island and jumped on the Crosstown bus at Thirty-Fourth Street and Seventh Avenue. I did not want to be late for my professional makeup appointment and was pleased the bus was waiting there when I reached Thirty-Fourth Street. I hopped on the crowded bus and politely made my way toward the back.

Before we even left the first stop, the bus driver screamed, "Does anyone know first aid?"

I jumped out of my seat and yelled, "I'm a nurse! Please let me through." As I reached the disabled seating in the front, I saw an elderly man slumped over in his seat and totally gray. I tried to get a pulse but couldn't. It was a struggle to get his dead weight to the ground with all the people crowding around us.

Once he was down, I knew he needed CPR if there was to be any chance of reviving him.

Instead of administering classic compressions, I was led to pinch his nose and blow the biggest breath into his mouth I possibly could.

Nothing happened.

Then I put my right hand on his chest, looked up to heaven and screamed, "Jesus!" Color instantly filled his face as he found himself looking at me as I sat on the floor next to him. I assured him an ambulance had been called and that he would be all right.

The whole bus seemed to spontaneously begin clapping. I turned around, pointed to heaven, and said, "Don't clap for me. Clap for Jesus."

Within moments, the ambulance arrived with EMTs. Everyone on the bus was transferred to another bus.

Two ladies lingered with me as I collected my belongings and said, "We knew you were a Christian because you didn't take the glory. You gave Jesus the glory. You need to testify at our church tonight."

I said, "Where do you go to church?"

They said, "Pastor Creflo A. Dollar."

"Great! That's where I go to church. I'll be there."

It was a wonderful night at the church, as usual.

Sometime later, word got out about this miraculous event and I was asked to do a taping recounting this event and other miracles I had witnessed.

Prophetic Word Comes True and Gold Dust Appears

In 1999, I was attending Village of Faith Church. During the service, the Lord kept prompting me to pray for a total stranger—a young man sitting with his two children.

During the service, the kids ran off to Sunday school and I jumped up and sat right next to him. I was sobbing uncontrollably.

He asked, "Are you all right?"

I said, "Yes! Can I pray with you at the end of service?"

He said, "Sure."

When the service ended, we made our way to the back of the church and held hands. I remember telling him, "Within this year, you are going to make ten times the amount of money you are making right now, owing to a huge promotion." Amen. There were other prophesies, but this was the big one. Naturally, he looked at me like I was a bit strange, but he politely said, "Amen." We exchanged numbers.

Months later, he called me and said, "Hey, prophet, you were right. The Lord blessed me on the job." We remained friends over the years.

Follow-Up

Recently, while attending a concert with a friend, we bumped into Dan. He told me that immediately after I prayed for him, when he walked into the lobby he felt as if he were floating and his feet were not touching the ground. People were coming up to him in the lobby asking him what the gold dust on his forehead was. He said he couldn't wipe it away that night. Praise the Lord!

Suicide Averted in Deli Mart

While on my way to do a private-duty case in East Hampton, I stopped at a 7-Eleven in South Hampton on Route 27 (Sunrise Highway) to grab a coffee to go. I had just pulled into a parking spot when my daughter, Annmarie, pulled up alongside me in the empty parking spot.

I was totally surprised and delighted to see her. We rolled our windows down simultaneously, and she said, "Come on, Mom; I'll treat you to a cup of coffee."

I thought, *Fabulous—what a wonderful surprise.*

All of a sudden, an overwhelming feeling of urgency came over me. As I was pulling out as fast as I could, I blurted out to my stunned daughter, "I have to go. I have to go!"

Annmarie yelled, "Where the heck are you going?"

The Holy Spirit was telling me I did not have a second to spare. I recklessly pulled out of the 7-Eleven parking lot and literally careened across the intersection. Good thing the Holy Spirit was driving.

I jumped out of the car and ran frantically into the deli mart to witness a tragic and unusual display by the cashier, who was crying uncontrollably and screaming, "Why am I still here? Why am I still here?"

The stunned line of patrons was standing there in shock.

I ran up to her behind the counter and threw my arms around her and kept saying, "God loves you."

She said, "You don't understand! If you had come in five minutes later, I was running home to take the rest of the bottle of sleeping pills to finish the job!"

I just kept hugging her and praying with her, telling her how much Jesus loves her and that she is needed. I said, "Your family needs you." Then her replacement came, and we walked to my car, talking, until I was sure her urge to kill herself had been repaired.

Follow-Up

Over time, she went back to church and school. The last time I saw her, she was a new version of herself, mentally and physically restored by our Lord.

Elderly Man Filled with Cancer Healed

One of my doctor's patients was scheduled to have surgery at 7:00 a.m. As a surgical nurse assistant, I had been moved by the Holy Spirit to meet with the mother, Erin, and her daughter, Tara, to pray with them before surgery around 6:00 a.m. I met them in the waiting room, sat down, held both their hands and said a little prayer for Tara.

As I looked up across the waiting room, I noticed an elderly couple sitting there quietly.

Erin looked at me and said, "Go ahead, Maria. I know what you have to do."

I slowly got up and went over to the wife and asked very softly, "Can I say a little prayer with you?"

She gave me a dismissive look and said, "My husband is filled with cancer."

I said, "I won't embarrass you, but can I say a little prayer?"

She reluctantly said, "Whatever."

I gingerly inserted myself between them and took both of their hands, silently praying for approximately sixty seconds. I said, "Amen," and I got up and left to go to work in the surgery center. Minutes later, the elderly man was taken to Surgery.

Approximately a half hour after I left, Erin informed me that the elderly woman had approached Erin, who was still waiting for her daughter's surgery to be finished.

She hysterically said, "She's an angel. Where is she? I need to find her! They opened my husband up, and there was no cancer in his body!"

Erin said, "That's my friend Maria. She is not an angel."

Word got around to the doctor I was working with, and he called me to say, "Maria, what are you trying to do—clear out Stony Brook Hospital?"

"No, but God is," I replied.

Several hours later, the surgeon returned. We continued to see patients, and at the end of the day he smiled at me and said, "I am going to make sure your phone number is on my speed dial."

Massive Cancerous Tumor in Stomach Disappears

One uneventful winter day, I walked into the Dollar Store in Rocky Point, Long Island, and was immediately struck by the unhinged behavior of one of their workers. He was running around the store proclaiming to anyone who would listen that he had been diagnosed with a massive tumor in his abdomen and was going in for an operation the next day.

It was understandable that anyone with this diagnosis would be freaked out the day before surgery. I found the manager and quietly asked if I could pray with Steve.

She said, "Yes, he is a mess. Go ahead."

With the permission of his manager, I found Steve in an aisle, stocking a shelf. I walked up to him and asked him if I could pray for him. Steve immediately started to express all of his fears and symptoms. He was beside himself in anticipation of the operation. Finally I just grabbed his hands and began to pray silently to myself while holding his hands.

Suddenly the Lord impressed me to tell him the diagnosis was a mistake. I just kept getting the words "It is a mistake!" These were definitely not *my* thoughts. I uttered, "It is a mistake!"

Steve kept saying, "They did two sonograms. I saw the tumor. The pictures don't lie!"

Still I held my ground, because Jesus just kept saying to me, "Tell him it is a mistake. It is a mistake." Frankly, I was thinking, "Wow, I'm really putting myself on the line here. Thanks a lot, Jesus!"

Finally I got his phone number, and I called him that night to pray with him, still claiming, "It is a mistake." I asked him to call me as soon as he got out of the operating room and let me know the good news.

Naturally, he said, "Yeah, right."

We hung up, and I went to bed.

The following day, late in the afternoon, I received a call from Steve's cell phone number, but there was a nurse on the other end. She told me that Steve was still groggy but he wanted her to tell me the doctors had said it was a mistake.

Whatever they had captured on sonogram was not there. They had absolutely no medical explanation for it except that it must have been a mistake.

"Thank you, Jesus," I replied.

Young Man Raised from the Dead

I was traveling home one spring Sunday after church when I came upon a scene that shocked me. A policewoman was kneeling over a body on the ground next to a flower stand.

I pulled over and ran out of the car toward the body.

The policewoman stated emphatically that he was dead. His shirt was wide open, and he looked totally gray.

I said, "I'm a nurse," as I knelt down beside him and her and saw how young he was. He was in his early twenties.

I cried out to the Lord, "Jesus, please don't let him die. He is too young!" I had my hands on his chest as I was literally crying over him.

Within a minute, his eyes opened. His color came back. I asked him his name.

He said his name was Saul.

I told him he was going to be okay.

I left the scene as the ambulance approached.

Shortly after, when I found a phone, I called the hospital I knew he had been taken to. I finally got through to the ER doctor to ask how Saul was doing and if I could visit him. I told him I was the nurse who had stopped by the side of the road.

The doctor paused a moment and said, “If you were a nurse, you would know the HIPAA law; we can’t release any information.”

I said, “Please, I just want to visit Saul.”

The doctor stated, “We discharged him; we couldn’t find anything wrong with him.”

I was in shock.

I have always wished that I would run into Saul again—but I never have.

Neighbor with Enormous Tumor Healed

My next-door neighbor Edie stopped by one night to say hi. She mentioned she was scheduled for surgery the following day to remove a grapefruit-sized tumor from her uterus. She was devastated at the prospect of losing this major organ and her femininity.

Being originally from Rotterdam in the Netherlands, she had an odd affinity for my background, because that's where my father was born. She really could not talk to her husband about this. I offered to pray with her. I held one of her hands and put the other on her stomach as I prayed. Edie began to laugh at me.

I said, "Jesus, do it any way you want. Thank you, Jesus; Edie is healed."

Then she put her hands on her hips and said, "Yeah, right. What is God going to do, take the tumor out on the operating table?"

I said, "Jesus can do it any way he wants."

She left. The next morning, around 5:30 a.m., as she was leaving for the hospital, I ran over to her house, gave her a hug, and said another quick prayer.

That night, her live-in exchange student surprised me by pounding on my front door. I answered it, and the girl said, "Edie needs your phone number. She needs to speak with you."

I gave it to her.

Within minutes, Edie was on the phone to me, exclaiming, "The doctors went in with the scope and only found scar tissue. I still have my uterus! I have to admit I thought you were crazy. But when you prayed, I felt heat go through my body. I thought it was my imagination. Thank you, Maria, for praying."

I said, "It was Jesus."

Deep Hole on Face Miraculously Healed

While I was working as a surgical nurse at a surgical center, one of our patients was a young, beautiful blonde girl about to get married. She had just had Mohs surgery (removal of cancer) several weeks prior, resulting in a deep hole which was on the side of her nose. She knew that it wouldn't be healed for her wedding. She was so depressed.

One of the doctors, who knew I was great at encouraging people, suggested I speak with the girl and her mother. He led me to a private office where they were sitting. I came in, and they both stood up. I was filled with compassion when I saw the depth of the hole.

The Holy Spirit in me compelled me to wrap my arms around the girl and pray. Her mother stood there in disbelief, watching the unusual behavior of a nurse. God only knows what she was thinking.

As I was hugging her and praying I was impressed to tell her that "God would close the hole and she would only have a pink little mark that she could cover with makeup for her wedding."

I thought the mother was going to kill me with her incredulous look. How could I give this frightened young girl false hope?

They both sat down.

I left the room, and the doctor entered to speak with them. After they left, the doctor found me standing in the hallway. "Maria, in my office now!"

As I entered, he scolded, "Shut the door and sit down. How could you give somebody false hope? You are a nurse. You should know better."

I responded, "I wasn't doing the talking. It was Jesus."

He shouted, "Get out! Get out of my office now."

Several weeks later, she came for her follow-up. As Jesus had promised, the hole was closed and was slightly pink in color. Makeup could very easily cover it for her wedding day. The mother told me she was sorry for doubting me, and they both hugged me.

Of course, I said, "It wasn't me. It was Jesus."

Follow-Up

Later on, the surgeon came in and stated, "Wow! I don't know what to say! I have seen you do this many times before, and I am amazed at the results your prayers produce."

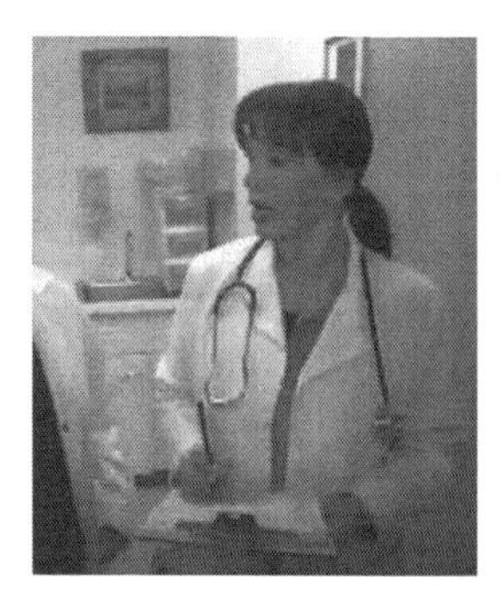

Maria in scrubs, working at surgi-center.

Three Miracles for Selena

Sometimes fate arranges circumstances that allow a relationship to flourish. Selena was finishing up in college and working as a teller at my bank four days a week back in 2015. Because I had a safe-deposit box, it allowed us to speak privately when I went into that room with her. Over time we shared a lot, and the Lord began to give me words for her. I didn't know it, but Selena was contemplating breaking up with her fiancé in 2017 when this occurred.

This particular day, as we were in the safe-deposit room, the Lord told me to tell her, "There will be a dramatic change—a turnaround. Everything will change. Saturday night He will give you a miracle."

I didn't know at the time that her relationship was crumbling and that she had spent many nights crying herself to sleep.

Selena told me that as she left to go home that Friday night, she felt lighter. However, by Saturday morning she was profoundly depressed again and felt her life was out of control. She decided to offer her fiancé an ultimatum. They met to talk it out, and she told him he had to either stay to work it out or leave her and the eight years they had shared behind.

Miraculously, he agreed to work things out. From that day, their relationship improved. She told me she thanked Jesus every day for that miracle.

Another time when I saw Selena at the bank, I was impressed to tell her the Lord wanted her to know she would be getting a new job with higher pay and more responsibility within a month. She had already been promoted from teller to assistant manager and was sitting at a desk. But the Lord told me she would be leaving the bank and her newly upgraded position to get a better one with higher pay, more benefits, and more responsibility at a different bank.

You cannot make this stuff up. She looked at me as if I were crazy. You would think she would have been be used to it by then.

Twenty-eight days later, when I stopped in the bank, she was no longer there. The Lord's prophetic word was exactly accurate, and she was thrilled as she told me in a text about her new position.

Very recently she was looking for a condo with her fiancé, and they had seen several. She sent me a picture of the condo they both loved.

The Lord said, "It's yours."

She said, "Yes, I'm doing exactly what you taught me to do. I'm thanking Jesus for it."

I told her she would be moving into the condo in two weeks. The very next day, she was notified they could move in within two weeks. It was very unusual for them to have such a short waiting period.

But, of course, Jesus was right again.

She said, "Now I'm telling everyone and anyone who will listen about Jesus."

Follow-Up

Selena is sharing the good news wherever she goes. All I can say is praise the Lord!

Severe Arthritis Miraculously Healed

While I was working as a surgical nurse, a woman with severe arthritis of the knee limped in to the office for a pre-op consultation. When I saw how much pain she was in, my heart went out to her and I asked if she would like me to say a little prayer with her.

As she limped down the hallway, she said, "Sure."

I sneaked her quietly into an empty office, which the staff had dubbed my "chapel." I placed my hand on her knee and prayed in the name of Jesus to take her pain away.

Immediately she said, "The pain is gone."

As we walked out of the office, she was no longer limping.

She exclaimed, "The pain is gone! Bye now." She walked out the door and never came back.

I was getting a reputation around the office that I was not good for business.

That's a good thing, as the people waiting for treatment no longer needed treatment because their diseases were healed.

Gastrointestinal Bleeding Stops after Prayer

During my rounds as a nurse in the surgical unit of a hospital on Long Island, I was visiting one of my patients that had had surgery the day before. As I spoke with her and prayed, the patient in the other bed overheard us and asked if I would pray with her. She was awaiting an exploratory operation of the abdomen to find out why she was bleeding internally. She had a nasal gastro tube that went into her stomach; it was pumping blood out while she waited for her operation. I said, "Sure," and I said a little prayer in the name of Jesus.

Before I left the room, the head nurse came in to tell her that the anesthesiologist was running late.

Half an hour later, I popped back into the room to check on both of them and noticed there was no blood in the tubing. The patient asked me whether it was her imagination or whether the bleeding had stopped.

I said, "No. It stopped. I don't see any blood coming out."

She said, "I have decided not to go ahead with the surgery."

I said softly to myself, "Oh boy," and I walked out of the room.

Before long, the anesthesiologist arrived at the patient's bedside, and I overheard him explain to her what he was about to do.

Before he finished, she abruptly told him, "I changed my mind. I'm not having surgery. I'm not bleeding. Look at the tubing; the bleeding stopped."

He was not happy and said she would have to speak with her surgeon. They made her sign a release.

The head nurse took me aside to reprimand me. She asked me if I had prayed for the patient.

I said yes.

She said it was unprofessional and that I was not supposed be bringing religion into the hospital.

I reminded her that the patient had stopped me and asked me to pray.

The patient was transferred to a nonsurgical floor and was still fine the next day when she was discharged. Jesus prevailed again!

Maria Baan, Actress

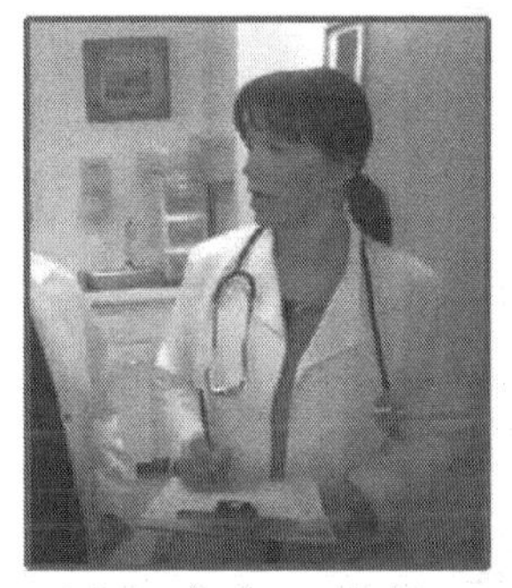

Maria playing a doctor.

Maria Baan

Maria as psychiatrist Dr. Sommersbond.

Businesswoman

Maria Baan.
Maria playing a doctor.
Maria as psychiatrist Dr. Sommersbond.
Businesswoman.

PART II

Miracles in the Entertainment Field

As I mentioned in the beginning of this book, I was smitten by every aspect of entertainment. You really can't beat a set (indoor or on location) for drama. That sounds like an obvious statement, but I mean it as much for what is going on with the director and the actors as I do for everything else that happens behind the scenes.

Set builders can literally be expected to build a house or dismantle one in a day. They are truly unsung heroes. Accidents can happen during filming that can cost thousands if the director or producer cannot substitute another scene to shoot. So you never know what to expect. It does not matter whether I'm on set as an actor or as a set nurse; God always uses me one way or another to make His presence known.

Miracles on the Movie *Bringing Out the Dead*

The first miracle in the entertainment field I experienced took place on the set of *Bringing Out the Dead*, directed by Martin Scorsese and starring Nicholas Cage. On *Bringing Out the Dead*, I worked as an actress and as a medical advisor.

Originally I was hired as an actress to play a resident doctor. Filming was at Bellevue Hospital, located in New York City. Once one of the assistant directors learned I was a nurse, he asked if I could give them my medical opinions on some of the scenes as a medical advisor.

I instructed Aida Turturro how to perform CPR and was asked what would be done if a person came into an emergency room with severe chest pain. The actor playing the patient having the chest pain was Vinny Vella. Vinny Vella was an actor who played mobsters and had a great sense of humor when not playing a part.

I prayed with several actors on the set and got the nickname "Angel." One of the actresses, an extra, was doubled over, obviously in excruciating pain, while waiting to do her scene. I walked over to her and sat next to her. I asked her, "Are you all right?"

She said she was experiencing extreme cramps.

I asked her if I could pray for her.

She said yes.

I put my arm around her, took her hand, and silently prayed. She jumped up, said she could feel heat coming from my hand, and said I prayed like her grandmother. The pain went away immediately.

Bringing Out the Dead was a great movie, and I was very excited to be involved with it. They frequently asked me if everything looked authentic, and it definitely did.

Disturbing Dream about Sylvester Stallone

Years after I worked with Sylvester Stallone as a hostage in *Nighthawks*, I woke up in the middle of the night sobbing, sitting up in my bed. All I kept getting was *Stallone, Stallone*. I knew something was wrong; I had to pray. It seemed as if I prayed for hours, but I am sure it was not long at all. The following day, it was everywhere in the news that while Stallone was filming *Rambo: First Blood Part II*, Stallone's FX specialist, Cliff Wenger Jr. had been working on a stunt explosion when it went horribly wrong. Sadly, he died instantly. It happened at the exact time the Lord woke me up to pray without ceasing. I believe Jesus kept Sylvester Stallone safe.

Sonny's Life Saved on the set of *Donnie Brasco*

Sonny and I were extras working on the movie *Donnie Brasco*, starring Al Pacino. I really did not want to work in this movie as an extra, but Jesus kept urging me to participate because of a miracle He wanted to perform. I knew that somebody could seriously get injured during the filming. I was in the green room when Sonny, a massive mafia type, approached me and asked me how I got the part. I told him, "The Lord gave me the part." He looked at me strangely for moment. I continued, "I'm here because I have to pray that someone does not get seriously injured."

Sonny mocked me saying, "Okay, Mother Theresa. What are you going to do without your rosary beads?" Then he shook his head as if I were nuts and walked out of the green room.

Suddenly I heard a crash and screaming. It was Sonny. I ran out. Sonny was on the ground holding his leg. He held back a macho tear in his eye as he said, "Who the hell are you? Something pushed me out of the way. I should have been pinned between the two cars that collided!" Then he said, "Jump in the car and check out the old guy who was driving to see if he is okay." Shortly thereafter, the ambulance came and took Sonny away.

Follow-Up

A few years later, when I worked with Sonny on another set, he confirmed that he had his leg broken that day, but he knew it should have been much worse. He smiled and said, "I feel so much better when you're around."

I looked up and said, "When *Jesus* is around."

Young Crew Member's Life Saved

While working as a set nurse on a very popular action TV series, the Holy Spirit directed me to examine a young production assistant (PA). I was prompted to ask an energetic, healthy-looking guy in his early twenties if he was okay. He said, "I'm okay." I gently insisted that he just humor me and let me take his vitals.

We were filming outside at a park in Brooklyn. I got him to sit down on one of the benches and took his pulse, which was irregular. Then I took his blood pressure, which was extremely low. He agreed to take a break for ten or fifteen minutes.

When I took his vital signs again, I had a bad feeling. The director noticed what was going on and told the PA that it was my call for what he should do. One of the young female PAs said she would go with him to the ambulatory walk-in clinic. So they did just that.

After several hours had passed and we had not heard anything, I was concerned. Finally the news came back that the clinic had sent him to a cardiac facility and told him, "Whoever sent you here saved your life."

I thought to myself, "Thank you, Jesus!"

Follow-Up

Within a few weeks, he was healthy and back to work.

Detached Fingertip Reattached without Stitches

While working as a nurse on a set construction job for a Netflix series, I was taken by surprise when the cleaning lady approached me with blood gushing from her index finger on her right hand. She had cut the tip of her finger almost completely off as she was cleaning set knives in the kitchen. It was literally a separate piece of flesh hanging by a thread of skin. Good thing I can stand the sight of blood. I immediately cleaned it and applied a pressure dressing while I was praying on her. I knew that in the natural she needed to go the ER and have it stitched back on.

She said she had to go to her next job, as her boss was picking her up.

As she left, I got her phone number and called her all weekend long to check on her. She never went to the ER, to my dismay.

Follow-Up

When she came to the set on Monday, I checked the finger, and miraculously the flesh had started to knit back together. I would call it a mini creative miracle. She is a Christian, so we both said, "Thank you, Jesus!"

God Cast Role on *The Sopranos*

My manager Jay called to tell me I had an audition for the role of Fran on *The Sopranos* on HBO. Fran was the girlfriend of Robert Loggia, who played Feech La Manna.

I told Jay, "That has to be a mistake. I prayed that my friend Delores would get that part."

"Well, I guess God didn't answer your prayer. Don't worry; she'll get a bigger part," Jay said.

"No, I can't go," I said.

"You have to be at Silvercup Studios tomorrow at 2:00 p.m.. Be there!"

I got the part. We filmed on April 6 at an exclusive restaurant in Brooklyn, New York. The scene was a bunch of mobsters sitting around a table out for dinner with their girlfriends.

I was sitting next to Robert Loggia, and he started to confide in me. "All my older friends are dying," he said. Then he remarked, "I can't believe I am sharing this with a total stranger."

"I am going to pray with you; that's why I am here," I told him.

"What! In front of everybody?" he asked incredulously.

"Well, in this scene we are supposed to be hugging and kissing, so as the camera goes around to the others hugging and kissing,

I'll be silently praying in your ear." Robert Loggia was stunned, but I proceeded to do just that.

As we were filming, the spirit of laughter overtook James Gandolfini, Robert Loggia, and me. Simultaneously we all burst out laughing and couldn't stop. There wasn't anything in particular that we found funny. It was just spontaneous.

Tim Van Patten, the director, came over to the table and asked, "Do you think we'll finish this scene?"

We got serious and finished the scene, holding back the spirit of joy and laughter.

At the wrap party, Robert's wife mentioned to me that Robert told her about me. I knew in my heart that the Lord had dealt with his fears.

In 2012 he played Peter in *Apostle Peter and the Last Supper.* Robert went home to the Lord in 2015.

When I thought about how this role came to me after I prayed fervently for someone else to get it, I realized I had to be there for Robert.

Miracle on *A Walk Among the Tombstones*

My job as a set nurse on *A Walk among the Tombstones*, starring Liam Neeson, was anything but boring. Around 3:00 a.m. one night, we were filming around a large pond at Green-Wood Cemetery in Brooklyn at the end of March. As I was trying to keep warm, a frantic call came over my walkie-talkie. "Medic, someone's throat is closing up!" I ripped off my coat to lighten my load because I had to fly around a large pond to get to the other side, where one of the young crew members needed help. I ran as fast as I could through wet leaves and bushes, with tree branches hitting me in the face.

When I arrived at the location on the other side, the young guy was standing there with his hand on his throat in distress. I asked him a few pertinent questions to assess his condition. He was very allergic to peas and they were in the soup he had eaten. I reached into one of my pockets and gave him a shot glass of liquid Benadryl, and while he drank it, I put my arm around him, which freaked him out a little. He asked, "What are you doing?"

I'm sure you already know what I said.

"I'm praying on you in the name of Jesus."

He looked at me like I was nuts and said, "Whatever works." Within seconds, he said, "I'm feeling better. I can swallow."

I absolutely knew the Benadryl could not work that fast. I stayed near him for the rest of the shooting that night, but he was really fine after the first few minutes. Thank you, Jesus!

Prophetic Word on the movie *Run All Night*

Jesus compelled me to accept a one-day set nurse job for some filming taking place three hours away from my home. Normally I would not have taken it. As usual, I was arguing with Him in my mind during the whole trip to the set location in Putnam County. As I walked on the set, I was met by highly agitated production assistants. They instructed me to go immediately to the trailer of Genesis Rodriguez, starring as Gabriela Conlon, Liam Neeson's daughter-in-law in the movie.

As I headed toward the trailer, it seemed as if the entire crew was shouting. "You have to help her," I heard someone say. "She needs something for her stomach. She has to do this scene today. We are on a schedule."

As I got closer to her trailer, a crew member I recognized from another project ran over to me and said, "She is sick over the death of Paul Walker."

I started to cry and thought, *Lord, why am I here?*

The Lord told me, "Tell her Paul is in heaven with Me."

I knocked on the door. Genesis opened it and asked me if I was the medic.

I said, "I'm the nurse," as I stepped into the trailer. I was compelled to hug her, and I said, "Jesus told me to tell you, 'Paul is in heaven with Me.'"

She said, "Oh my God. You are a Christian! I prayed this morning that God would give me a sign that Paul is in heaven."

We cried together for a few minutes as I wiped the tears from her eyes and mine. I then said, "Come on; you can do this." We held hands and walked out of the trailer.

The Lord propped her up to finish her work on the set. At every break, she came to me, and we huddled together until the end of the shoot that day. When she was finished with her scenes for the day, her car came, and the crew kept yelling, "Let's go. Your car is waiting."

Genesis said, "You'll be here tomorrow, right?"

I said, "No, I was just filling in today. You know why I was here today. The Lord wanted me to give you that message."

She said, "Hollywood needs you. We need you on the front line."

We hugged and I said, "I'll see you again."

Follow-Up

I do believe I will see her again, but I haven't yet.

Multiple Miracles on Rap TV Show

Over the course of six to eight weeks, I was hired as a set nurse usually three or four times a week while they were filming a series on rap's golden age. The theme was centered on urban kids trying to break into the industry, much as they are today. Needless to say, the normal language of the rappers could burn one's ears. I kept asking Jesus, "Do you really want me on this set?" It was a bit out of my comfort zone. The kids were terrific, even if the language was strong. We shot at a number of different locations—mostly the boroughs of New York City.

I was on high alert regarding all the stunt work called for in the script. One particular day, a stunt person was scripted to tumble down an outside wooden stairway onto leaf-covered concrete in Ozone Park.

At the time scheduled to film this stunt, torrential rain was falling. The stunt coordinator and I knew we needed to hold off filming because of the danger. The Lord told me to tell them to hold off for ten minutes and the rain would stop. When I told the stunt coordinator to ask for ten minutes, he was a bit dubious that would be all the delay we needed. The crew outright mocked me when they heard what I said. You can't blame them.

So I stepped out into the middle of the street, pointed to the sky and said out loud, "Jesus, stop the rain like you did on the boat with the disciples!"

The crew howled. "The medic has lost it!" someone said. "What drug are you on?" Within less than ten minutes, the rain completely stopped.

Someone joked, "What are you going to do next, part the Red Sea?"

I said, "No. That was Moses."

Then I was prompted to say, "Would you like to see the sun? Look up." Out of a completely overcast gray sky, the sun popped out like magic. That seemed to raise an eyebrow or two.

And then I said, "Would you like to see a rainbow?" Look up now, because there is going to be a tiny rainbow, but it will not last very long." Instantly, a perfect, tiny, classic rainbow appeared for a few seconds. Some were speechless, seemingly in shock, and others walked away shaking their heads. But I'm used to it.

At another location, inside a huge indoor studio after they had called, "It's a wrap!" I received a bloodcurdling scream over my walkie-talkie. I then heard "Maria! Get to the men's room now!"

I ran up two flights of stairs to the wrong men's room. When I got there, I was directed to the other men's room on the other side of the set, up another flight of stairs.

I ran down the two flights, across the entire set, and up the other flight of stairs as fast as I could. I think the angels must have sped me along because the need was great.

When I got to the correct men's bathroom I was greeted by one of the producers, who was holding the door open. In a panic, he said, "Maria, he's dying! You have to do something! He's choking!" One of the 6'2" producers was literally choking to death, turning blue and gurgling.

I put my arms around him as best I could as he unintentionally fought me in his panic. I attempted the Heimlich maneuver three times, to no avail. The fourth time, I looked up and yelled, "Jesus, You saved my life when I was choking. Jesus, I need Your help now!"

With the fourth attempt, a chicken bone flew out of his mouth. The other producer said, "Amen, sister, and he high-fived me.

Just in case you were wondering, I'm 5'4". Doing the Heimlich maneuver on someone much taller than yourself is very challenging.

I sat the choking victim on a chair, and he kept repeating, "You saved my life."

Of course, I declared, "No, Jesus saved your life."

PART III

Me, a Grandmother?

I was thirty-nine going on forty when I became a grandmother for the first time. The thought of being called "Grandma" by anyone in public made me feel old. However, when Luis Michael and Gabrielle were born, the euphoria was overwhelming.

I spent a blessed and considerable amount of time helping to raise them. Annmarie was going to nursing school, and much like when I was a single mother, I needed all the help I could get. It was the delight of my life to be in their lives as much as I could.

Our Trip to Disney World and Discovery Cove

One particular miraculous time, when they were seven and three, I was able to take Luis and Gabrielle to Florida to visit Disney World and Discovery Cove. Disney World was great, but Discovery Cove was very accurately called "A Day in Paradise." We never wanted to leave the dolphins; we had fallen in love with them. Thank goodness we took plenty of photographs to look back on.

Luis Michael, Gabrielle and me enjoying the dolphin.

Luis and I got to ride the dolphin, but Gabby, being too young, had to settle with just kissing the dolphin. However, this was beyond her expectations. Luis and Gabrielle had always been animal lovers. These moments embedded profound images and experiences that would live in our memories forever. Little did I know or suspect that this transformative vacation would be the last we would all spend together in such unbridled bliss.

Gabrielle kissing a dolphin.

The Joy of Being a Grandmother

As a toddler, Luis, like his sister, was too beautiful for words. Strangers would notice him and comment every time I was in public with him. He was precocious and curious. He loved and charmed everyone. Women would come up to me and comment about his big brown eyes and how they wished they had his eyelashes, which touched his eyebrows.

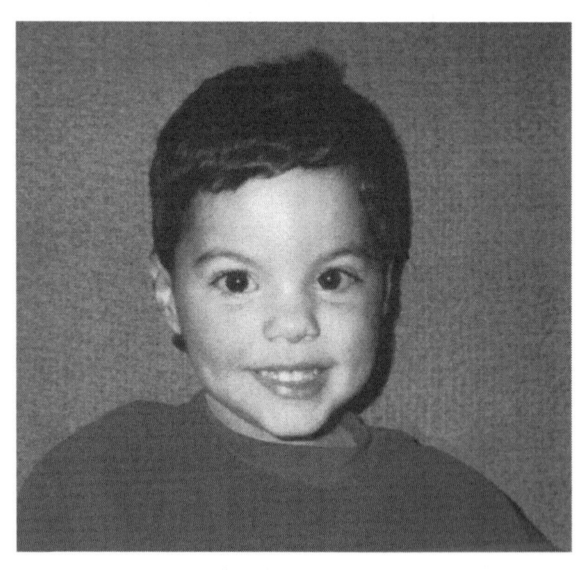

Luis Michael at two years old.

In school he excelled and was bored by less-than-challenging curricula. You could say he was as rambunctious as he was curious.

Around seven or eight years old, Luis Michael started going with me to volunteer at soup kitchens around the major holidays, such as Thanksgiving and Christmas. He loved serving the people, and they loved him. It was delightful to witness his genuine love for helping people at such a young age.

Luis Michael and Maria.

Raising My Grandchildren

Around the ages of sixteen and twelve, Luis Michael and Gabrielle would also enthusiastically accompany me during the Christmas holiday to sing at nursing homes where their mother and I sometimes worked.

A spark to help the elderly was ignited in Luis Michael that only grew stronger as time went on. During one holiday caroling excursion, Luis Michael noticed an elderly woman struggling to feed herself during a meal. He immediately bolted over to assist the woman in feeding herself and was reprimanded for doing so. They called him into the nursing office to instruct him on proper protocols, and he responded indignantly, "No one else was helping her at the time, so I'll just have to get a job here." And he did; approximately a year later, he got a job working at the same nursing home, thanks to his mother. How many eighteen-year-old boys do any of us know that would be passionately drawn to work with the elderly?

Luis Michael and elderly patient.

Our Holiday Tradition

From the time my daughter and grandchildren were young, during the Christmas season, I would take them to see the tree at Rockefeller Center.

On our trips to Rockefeller Center, we took tons of photos.

We truly enjoyed ice skating—or at least they did. Ice skating was not my forte. I took a hard fall and decided to sit on the sideline and watch them enjoy themselves.

We would then make our way to Little Italy for dinner.

On the train ride home, all they did was talk about how much fun they had.

Granny on the Run

(Written by Gabrielle)

My grandma took my boyfriend and me to the city, and it's never boring with my granny. We were just walking down the road to get to Little Italy to get some dinner, while people approached us with offers and flyers.

My response to all these offers was "No, no, no, and no."

A woman came up to me and said she did palm readings.

I rolled my eyes, said, "No thanks," and walked away with my boyfriend.

My Boyfriend and I were walking and suddenly felt it was too quiet and began wondering where Granny was.

And of course, she was talking to the "psychic." I was over on the side like, "Oh my God, Granny, come on; I'm hungry. She needs Jesus, and we all know that; let's leave!" Before I knew it, Granny was talking, and the woman started crying. My Boyfriend and I looked at each other like, "What the heck is going on?"

Ten minutes later, they were still talking, and the woman was still crying. While Granny was hugging this stranger, I was thinking, *Uh oh, Granny changed her life.* My Boyfriend was just thinking, *That's typical*, and twenty minutes later we were still waiting for Granny. I saw granny and the woman hug good-bye and exchange phone numbers.

We walked maybe half a block, and all I saw was a man go flying in the air. I ran over and saw a man on the ground.

I started yelling to Granny that she needed to run over here and help. So she started running down the block with her huge purse. My Boyfriend was speechless, and I was yelling, "Hurry up!" She ran over and asked the man questions and began trying to help.

Granny removed her scarf and made a sling to keep his arm and shoulder stabilized so he wouldn't cause further damage. She was asking the guy questions and praying on him—of course—and asking if he knew God. My Boyfriend and I were just standing there trying to help in any way possible.

Then the undercover EMTs showed up.

Seeing stuff like that where my granny helps people on the street—not just at work, but anywhere—is really the reason why I want to be in the medical field.

Watching my grandma help people without being prepared or anything—just seeing her know exactly what to do—it blows my mind, and it's amazing to watch how my grandma changes people's lives all the time.

Heartwrenching Prophetic Word about Sylvester Stallone's Son and My Grandson

For about six months before this tragedy, I kept getting, in my spirit, *Stallone, Stallone, Stallone.*

I asked God, "What? What about Stallone?"

The Lord said, "You're going to see Sylvester Stallone again."

I thought to myself, *Okay, he does his own stunt work; I'll work as a nurse on the set.*

All of a sudden, the Lord said, "No, you're an actress, and you're going to give him a message: his son is with Me in heaven."

I cried.

About six months later, I received a call from my daughter that Luis Michael was in the ICU. I immediately drove to the hospital. I entered the parking lot of the hospital knowing my grandson was in critical condition.

As I was turning off the ignition, the presence of Jesus filled the car. I heard the Lord say, "You are going to tell Stallone his son is with your grandson with me in heaven. I begged the Lord, "No! I'll tell Stallone anything, but not that!"

Stunned, I wiped away the tears and ran into the hospital and up to the front desk. They informed me that I was not next of kin and that they had to call security down to get permission for me to go up to the ICU. Within a couple of minutes, the security guard arrived and he introduced himself. He told me his name was Rocky. At that moment, I collapsed to my knees, sobbing. I knew it was another sign from God confirming the tragic prophetic word I had been given a few minutes earlier in the car.

They brought me upstairs to Luis Michael's bedside. I was in a state of shock as I stood outside the room. Because I'm a nurse, I instantly realized he was being kept alive by all the life-support machines. My daughter was at the bedside, weeping. The hospital chaplain approached to console me and said, "Luis was given last rites in the emergency room."

I was still in profound denial and blurted out, "I don't care what they gave him. I have seen three people raised from the dead, so I'm not listening to you."

In my heart, I knew as I proceeded into the room that this prophetic word would come true.

Leaning over the side railing, I kissed Luis on the cheek and whispered, "I love you, and I need you, and Jesus loves you." Unable to contain my emotions, I immediately left for home.

As my head hit the pillow, I was still begging Jesus to not take Luis Michael.

At 5:00 a.m., I bolted upright in the bed, and at 5:01 a.m., my daughter, Annmarie, called me and said, "Luis Michael is gone."

I truly believe that Luis got a glimpse of heaven and chose heaven. One of my best friends called me later that day with the exact same message.

Important note: A word to the wise when visiting anyone in a hospital who appears to be comatose: be very cautious how you speak anywhere near the patient. Countless times people have awoken to repeat what they heard while they were supposedly in a coma. Words can heal, and words can kill.

As a matter of fact, Pastor Perry Stone informs us that hearing is the last sense that shuts down on a dying person.

Everyday Miracles

Miracles are all around us: a newborn baby crying for the first time, the innocence of a child, the sun coming up, and the stars in the sky.

Even when we're running late, stuck in traffic, and getting ourselves agitated, only to find out later on that there was a major accident which we could easily have been involved in had we left at our usual time—this is a miracle in itself.

Miracles come in all forms, large and small, seen and unseen.

After reading this book, take a look around and really see the miracles that surround you. You need only believe to have a free gift that will last forever. Call on Jesus Christ to be your Lord and Savior. He loves you just as you are.

In memory of Luis Michael
1990–2017

Until we meet again—
I will always love you

In Gratitude

I praise the Lord for leading me to Community of Christ Healing Center in Rocky Point, New York. Pastors Dan and Kathy Holohan are the angels that were there for me at the time of the most difficult event in my life—the loss of my beloved grandson, Luis Michael. They continue to be an inspiration, and I thank God for them every day.

Prior to being a member of the church with Pastor Dan Holohan, I belonged to World Changers with Pastor Creflo and Pastor Taffi Dollar. They truly taught me so much about faith, and I am still a partner. Learning about faith and God's grace has changed my life.